Little Miss Excitement
Inspired by Erika

By Guy Marini

Illustrations by Tom Arvis

Dedication:

My Little Miss Excitement's story didn't end with that home run. As a high school & college athlete, she was named to All State's teams and was a Regional All-American in college.

The joy of Erika goes way beyond her athletic exploits. She is uniquely big hearted and brings happiness to literally all whose lives she touches.   During a significant difficult event in her young life, she rallied her friends & teammates through a tragedy. To see her selflessness in that time proved to all that she was an old soul with a big heart.

Finally, her zest for life & fun is infectious. Erika, this book is dedicated to you!

So M.L and Guy finished a nice dinner. Yes, you know it, M.L. made some delicious home made white pizza. (No tomato sauce – you have to try it sometime.)

The stork was soon to deliver us our third child and Mama M.L., Brother Matt, Sister Danielle and Dad Guy were all pretty anxious.

The stork was due to arrive on Thanksgiving Day, November 28, 1985.

Well, we had turkey, mashed potatoes and yes...just a little pizza for Guy, and we waited.

So while we enjoyed the love of our family and had yummy food, we kept looking out the window for the stork. I thought I saw it but it turned out to be a big beautiful bird flying south for the winter.

So we waited, waited and waited and finally on December 2, 1985 the stork showed up but not in the hospital!!

He showed up and dropped a beautiful, smiley baby girl into M.L.'s lap at 1 AM in the morning!

Yikes – what do we do!! No doctor, no nurse, no hospital... only my M.L., a very nervous new father, Guy, and our new little baby girl.

So Mama M.L. was calm and the new baby was smiling. Well – they seemed to have the situation under control.

Guy ran up and down the stairs calling doctors, nurses, hospitals, the police and fire department.

Guy ran around like he got stung by 500 bees – nuts, frantic, and pretty goofy...luckily Mama M.L. and Erika knew what to do.

So we did get through that adventure thanks to Mama M.L., Baby Erika, the fire department, the doctor, the nurses and the police.

The fireman who came to the house said, "Her name should be Little Miss Excitement". What a wild and crazy delivery!!

Guy also, finally calmed down and when asked about how he dealt with the stork's delivery, he sort of told a little different story then what really happened. He almost made it sound like he was in control and in charge. Let's say he was a bit confused by it all.

Soon, thereafter, Erika became the apple of everyone's eye...full of fun, a mischievous grin and the biggest most beautiful smile you ever did see!

Everything was exciting with her...even a simple morning breakfast...

It went like this...Erika in a high chair, with her baseball cap on sideways, diaper, no socks, no pants, no shirt. Her favorite was cereal with applesauce and bananas.

The only problem was everyone around was wearing it...in their hair, on their faces, on their clothes, on the walls.

All the while Baby Erika hooted and hollered and giggled through it.

So one day, I had to get tough...she looked sad...dropped her chin to her chest...ate a few bites and then started to store the food in her cheeks and finally squirted it out all over her Dad's big nose and moustache! What a mess!!

One day while sitting in her baby mobile walker, she looked down the stairs and saw some of her siblings toys. She must have wondered how she could get them.

   She was thinking…"Can't get out of the chair without help?
Don't want to bother Mom and Dad or my brother and
sister. Hey, how about I just take this mobile walker down the
stairs!!"

   Dad was cutting the grass and Mom was doing laundry
when we heard this boom, ba-boom sound and something
that sounded like "YEE-HAH". We rushed to find Erika in
her mobile at the bottom of the stairs on it's side and her
reaching for the toys, cooing at us and smiling and giving us a
little thumbs up.

11

In a few short months winter came and it snowed and snowed and snowed.

Her brother and sister dressed to go outside and go to the big hill across the street from our house to go sledding. Well, while Baby Erika was pretty tiny she decided she needed to go. So Mom bundled her up...she looked like a little snowman with her hazel eyes, button nose and cute little smile. We took our beloved golden retriever R.J. with us too. R.J. just loved snow!

What a blast we had! There were so many kids and parents outside. Everyone was talking and laughing and sledding pretty fast down the hill.

I was taking Baby Erika down little hills while her brother and sister were going down the big hills. Little Erika gave me this look like "Hey big guy, you can go down little hills – the big hills are calling me."

One of my neighbors called me over for a chat – little Erika at my side.

   As my neighbor and I talked about the sledding, the weather and work – Erika drifted out to find her brother and sister... and, soon thereafter... Erika was sledding down the hill laying on top of her sister and brother with R.J. sitting on Baby Erika.

   They went down the hill with shouts of glee, got to the bottom and rolled off into deep snow powder. As I ran down the hill I fell on my bottom and slid down the hill out of control.

14

Soon I landed in a pile of snow right next to Matt, Danielle, R.J. and Erika...all laughing at their poor, old, clumsy Dad. When I asked who came up with the idea to take three kids and a dog down the hill on a sled, they all pointed to Erika who gave me a cute, mischievous smile and a shoulder shrug.

So I like to have a little fun too. As I looked at them at the bottom of the hill, I could see they were wondering if I was going to get mad and take them home.

I told them I had an idea...

We went back up the hill and I laid on the sled and said, "Hop on guys – here we go!"

I don't know how... but we slid down that hill and went further than anyone had gone that day. When we stopped, I rolled over and we all tumbled in the snow.

We came out laughing and smiling and everyone was cheering for us; but, by that time we were a little cold.

  So I said, "Kids, how about we head home for a little bit of hot chocolate!"

  Erika looked at me, hugged our puppy R.J., and said "Can R.J. have some too?!"

We all looked at each other and smiled and said, "Of course, Little Miss Excitement."

As Erika got older, Mama M.L. asked, "Erika, would you like to try ballet?" You see, Erika was tiny and athletic. Well, she tried it but the tights, ballet slippers, and the outfits were not to her liking.

She said, "How about I play baseball with my brother?"

Mama M.L. and I shared with her that little girls do sports like tennis, softball...you know, things like that."

She said, "OK, I would like to try softball."

Well, the softball players did their hair, wore ribbons, and performed rhythmic chants on the field. The bat bags had to have the same colors as the uniform.

After one game, Erika looked at me and said, "This is like a ballet recital with a glove on. It's time for me to try baseball. What do you say Dad? If I do one more chant, I may run off the field singing "take me out of this soft ball game.""!!!

After a discussion with Mama Marini, we said, "O.K., baseball it is, Erika."

Well, she got picked for a team but the coaches did not know what to do with her...so they let her play two innings a game in the outfield. She was disappointed and patient.

Then it happened, a little guy hit a long fly ball to right field and she ran back and made a great catch to end the game. Her teammates on the field went nuts as did the fans as she ran in from the outfield with the ball in her glove.

A woman looked at me and said, "Wow, she's Little Miss Excitement, isn't she!!" I thought about the stork story... the mess she made when she ate...the trip down the stairs in her mobile...the sledding on top of her brother and sister with our dog. This catch she made to end the game and said, "Yup, that's what we've always called her-- "Little Miss Excitement!"

Little Miss Excitement didn't stop there.

The baseball coaches figured out she could play and help the team. She became one of the best players in the whole league – played on the All-Star team and one day became the only little girl to hit a home run over the fence. Local legend has it that the ball is still flying in the air somewhere.

I will end this book with a question for you. When your parents, friends, grandparents, aunts and uncles think of you, do they have a nickname for you? If so, what is it and why do they call you that? If you don't have a nickname, what would you like it to be and why?

Draw a picture about the story!

Other **Super Nonno** Books by Guy Marini Available on Amazon.com :
Super Nonno - The Adventures of Super Nonno
For The Love of Freckles
For The Love of Pizza
My Best Buddy M.L.
The Boy Who Loved Trucks
Patsy, Pipi & Duke

Made in the USA
Middletown, DE
31 March 2019